GULLY

Gull and Crossbones

By Jon Cleave

Published in 2008
© 2008 Jonathan Cleave

www.thegullery.co.uk

ISBN-10: 0-9553165-6-1
ISBN-13: 978-0-9553165-6-2

Design by Brad Waters www.bradwaters.com
Printed in the Westcountry by The Printing Press

For Ian and Cinders

It's good being a gull. You should try it. You'd get to do all sorts of naughty fun things. You know, pinching pasties and ice creams, screeching and squawking, dive bombing and splattting all over people's heads, all that sort of stuff.

It's brilliant!

Being a gull is the best!

Sometimes though, even I like a bit of a change and some days I pretend that I'm something else, just to keep life interesting.

On the particular day I'm going to tell you about, I was in a particularly *swashbuckling* mood.

Now there's a good word, swashbuckling. I'm not sure what it means, because I'm only a gull, right, but I think it might have something to do with.... *pirates*!

Do pirates swash and buckle, or do they buckle and squash? I don't know, but I simply had to find out what swashbuckling was all about, and there was only one way to do it. I had to become piratey for the day.

I stood on top of my chimney pot, high up in the gullery and gazed out to sea, and I sniffed the salty air and felt the warm sea breeze in my feathers, and I thought of pirate ships and a life on the ocean waves.

I was just stretching my wings like sails

I thought of pirate ships...

and preparing to launch for lunch, when I heard a little voice from the gullery below.

It was the princess.

'Gully,' she said. 'You're plotting something, I can tell.'

'I am swashbuckling today, that's all,' I said. 'I can't help it.'

'Can I be swashbuckling too?' she asked. 'Whatever that is.'

Well, I thought, what harm can it do? She could be my pirate princess.

'I suppose you can,' I said. 'Come on, let's go swashbuckling together!' We flapped up into the air and launched out over the village, in search of a piratey adventure and, of course, lunch.

We flew out over the beach, from where a lot of noise seemed to be coming.

Now normally when there's a lot of noise coming from the beach, it's because of one thing and one thing only. It's usually us gulls screeching and squawking and screaming and squabbling, not necessarily in that order, and usually over something vitally important like a stinky, smelly, rotten old haddock's head or a conger eel's tail, or perhaps a cheesey sandwich or a nasty pasty that one of my mates has pinched…whatever.

We all want a piece of it for ourselves, and in my experience the louder you shriek and squeal, the more likely you are to get some of it, or if you're very lucky, all of it.

We're gulls right? It's what we do.

I listened carefully, but it wasn't the pleasant and melodious sounds of lovely, handsome, beautiful gulls that I could hear. No, it was the horrid, ear splitting sound of fun and laughter, the sound of jollity and enjoyment. It was the sound of children playing a game of pirates.

On my beach!

There were quite a few children running around. Some were bigger than others and I didn't really recognise them at all. You all look alike to me anyway. But as I looked closer, one of them stood out.

His name was Tyrone Trumper.

The thing was, I hardly recognised him because he was doing something different to what he normally did. He wasn't playing on his XBoyGameBox thing or whatever it's called, or watching the gullyvision, or throwing stones at me and the princess, or being cheeky to lovely, nice, kind, sweet old Mrs Baker. No.

He wasn't generally skulking and sulking about the streets with his hood up over his head, covering his miserable face. No. He was playing with other children and laughing and having fun.

All right, when I say having fun, he was having fun because he was pretending to be the pirate king. He had a patch over his eye and a spotted scarf on his head, and an inflatable parrot on his shoulder, and he was making all the other smaller children walk the

Tyrone,
the Pirate King

'Walk the plank you scurvy dog!'
said Tyrone

'Jump down into the
whirlpool of doom!'

plank to their doom, along the jetty by the rock pools.

'Go on,' he shouted. 'Walk the plank you scurvy dog!'

He prodded a cute, curly headed child with his wooden cutlass, and the little one teetered towards the end of the jetty, where there was a small jump down into a sandy pool.

'Get on with it!' said Tyrone. 'I got others to drown yet, and some to stab and slash and maim a bit. Go on, you big baby! Jump down into the shark and jellyfish and croc infested whirlpool of doom!'

'No!' called back the little boy, arms folded in defiance. 'Shan't! I don't like smelly old jellyfish much and I ain't going to and you can't make me!'

Tyrone stopped enjoying himself. Things weren't going to plan.

He looked over to his mum and dad, Lionel and Honeysuckle, who were sitting plonked in the middle of a vast and colourful collection of beach paraphernalia.

There were deck chairs, kites, an inflatable lilo tied to a windbreak, beach towels, swimming trunks, shrimp nets, a beach umbrella, balls, boules, buckets and spades and everything you could possibly think of for the beach.

There was also the biggest picnic I had ever seen!

There were huge plastic bottles of deadly-sweet tooth-rotting cola coka from ValuCheeps, and flasks of sugary tea and coffee, and crisps and pies of every flavour, and biscuits and sandy sandwiches and pies with every conceivable filling, and boiled eggs and chicken drumsticks and squausages (which were like sausages, only Lionel had accidentally sat on them!) and pies and whole cooked chickens and stuff.

And, of course, there were pies. Did I mention the pies at all?

Wish you were here
♡ & Xxx's
The Trumpers

'Dad,' called Tyrone. 'That kiddie ain't playing fair. He won't jump into the whirlpool of doom like what I'm telling him to.'

The other children were lined up on the jetty, waiting to be prodded to their whirling, swirling doom, and beginning to look a little bored..

'Play nicely, our Tyrone,' said Honeysuckle. 'He's only little. Sing him a pirate song or something.......

What shall we do with the drunken sailor?

Early in the morning.

Hooray, up she rises,

Hooray up she rises,

Hooray...'

'Avast behind, hush that row!' shouted Lionel at Honeysuckle.

'That ain't very nice, my love,' she said.

'Trying to get the boy to sing, you'll turn him into a cissy! Go on, our Tyrone, prod the nasty little twit off the end with your cutlass. No mercy. You're pirate king, right?'

Lionel bit into a pie, opened a monster bag of crisps, glugged some cola coka from a bottle, stuffed a few sandwiches into his hamstery cheeks, and chose himself a chocolate biscuit from a large tin, then another, then another, and slammed them into his mouth all at the same time.

I had to admire Lionel's style! I think that he could have made quite a good seagull, because he's certainly greedy enough!

The little chap jumped off the end of the jetty into the sandy-bottomed pool and splashed and jumped around, laughing and whooping. The others, still lined up behind

Tyrone, were now more bored than ever.

'Oi!' shouted Tyrone. 'You got to roll around in agony now, while the sharks chew your legs off and the croc gets your head in his mouth and does the underwater crocodile death roll with you, and then them poisonous jellyfish stings you all over!'

The little boy just splished and splashed and splooshed up and down in the pool, and the others jumped in and joined him.

'Nah, nah! Nah, nah! There's no smelly old jellyfish in this pool! Nah, nah!' they shouted.

Tyrone snivelled and whinged and stomped back to Honeysuckle, who wrapped him in a towel.

'The thing is my darling, you can't *make* them other kiddies do what you want,' she said kindly.

Lionel frowned. 'Course he can. He's pirate king, right! He can do what he likes to 'em! Do you want me to go over and make 'em pretend there's poisonous jellyfish and piranhas and sea snakes and stuff? Or shall daddy go to that aquarium and get you some real ones to put in there?'

'No you shan't,' said Honeysuckle firmly.

'Oi, don't you get all hoighty-toighty with me,' said Lionel. 'I'm just parenting, that's all. Trying to be a good father to the boy.'

'Now Tyrone,' said Honeysuckle. ' Have something from the picnic to cheer you up. What about ….'

'He don't want no picnic my love. Go get the boy a take-away, something good for him like a burger or chips or something. He don't want none of this!' said Lionel, cradling his food with his plump arms and obviously not wanting to share anything.

Honeysuckle gave up. She got Tyrone to his feet, and took him off to the take-away. Lionel lay down on the lilo, and within minutes he was fast asleep and snoring like a hog.

A very big hog.

Watching Lionel had made me and the princess a little hungry-ish, a tad famished, a little peckish.

You see, it was my lunchtime now and we always try to eat at around one-ish.

Well to be honest, we always try to eat at two-ish as well.

Well yes, and three-ish….and if truth be known four-ish and five-ish too.

Anytime at all, in fact, is lunchtime-ish for us.

I must say, the princess and I quite fancied a nice picnic too. One just like Lionel's, in every detail, would do nicely. And, I thought, what on earth is the point in looking around for another picnic exactly the same as Lionel's when his was spread out so conveniently for us?

We landed on the beach and sauntered around and around, and took a good look. There was a vast selection of goodies on display at Lionel's picnic, and my beak was positively watering with hunger.

Now I'm not one to use the 'S' word, but it did begin to look like we might have to *share* the picnic, because we were joined at the forthcoming feast by a bird we knew as the beach master, the hideous Black Annie.

She was a huge evil-looking, one-eyed gull, with a beak like a cutlass. She'd lost a leg in a fight with a dog, and she had big black wings that hung over her like a vampire's cloak. She hopped along the shoreline all day long looking for scraps of fish and stuff, and terrified all the other gulls that came near her.

In turn, the three of us were joined by Snitch and Snatch, a pair of squabbling squabs who had just learned to fly, and who were making a dreadful nuisance of themselves all over the village. Their behaviour was, frankly, appalling…even by seagull standards!

We circled Lionel. I could tell that Black Annie had her eye on a pie, and Snitch and Snatch had theirs on the family-sized packet of crisps. For my part, I thought the princess and I could go Italian, and I had my eye on a delicious strand of spaghetti that tied the lilo to the windbreak.

Lionel was fast asleep and snoring!

Lionel lay sprawled, snorting and snoring on the lilo, rather like a whale who'd lost his way and become beached ashore.

Carefully I went over and gave the spaghetti a tug.

It came away easily. There was loads of it and I began to swallow from one end, while the princess began from the other. As we swallowed, we got closer and closer to one another until, how romantic, we ended up beak to beak.

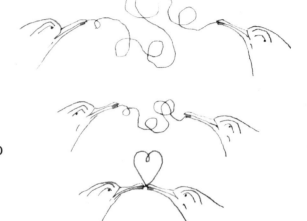

How I love her….

She was looking a bit sick though and I have to tell you that it didn't taste too good, in fact it didn't taste of anything much at all really.

It wasn't until I saw Black Annie looking sideways at me with her good eye and laughing that I realised it wasn't spaghetti after all.

How romantic!

It was a stupid piece of string.

What a blinking swizzle!

We left the stupid swizzle of string on top of Lionel's belly, pinched a sandy sandwich each, and flew off out over the harbour, and landed on a floating piece of driftwood and began to eat them.

Very soon, we were joined by Snitch and Snatch, who squabbled and squawked and screeched and ripped and tore open the crisp bag, so that the crisps flew everywhere, and while Snitch ate the crisps, Snatch tried to eat the bag.

Then Black Annie glided in on her big black vampire wings with what looked like a whole cooked chicken in her beak, though we were all a bit too scared to get close up and take a look, and we bobbed and bobbled about in the harbour on the piece of driftwood, nibbling our floating picnics, and wondering what we should pinch next.

There we are, nibbling our picnics...

Lionel was in a deep, deep sleep. He was dreaming a dream, and because it was Lionel it was a big, fat, greedy dream, a dream of a pirate life on the high seas, of cruel Captain Lionel aboard his ship the Saucy Squausage.

No one ever had such a delicious dream, because Lionel was dreaming of eating his pirate booty, a treasure trove of chocolate, sweets and pieces of cake captured from his enemies. He smacked his lips and drooled and dribbled all over the lilo, and thrashed his head from side to side in a frenzy of dreamy gluttony.

The dream felt so real to Lionel. It was almost as if he was actually sailing, actually floating on the water.

If I'm honest, that's probably because he was floating on the water!

You see, that piece of spaghetti, that stupid swizzle of string, the one that I had untied and tried to eat with the princess and then regurgitated in favour of a sandy sandwich? Well, that had turned out to be the piece of string that had tied the inflatable lilo to the windbreak.

And Lionel was still lying on the lilo!

Unfortunately, now the tide had come in and Lionel and the lilo (the Saucy Squausage of his dream), and all the other bits and bods of his beach stuff *and* the picnic were afloat on the sea.

Bye, bye Lionel - enjoy your voyage!

We watched from our piece of driftwood as the breeze gently blew the brightly coloured beachy flotilla, Lionel and the lilo away from the beach, and away past us!

Lionel, still greedy dreaming of a wicked life on the ocean waves, floated out between the harbour walls, past the high cliffs and fields that led down to the headland and off out to sea.

It had not escaped our notice that on board the Saucy Squausage was a large stash of treasure. Lionel's picnic was spread all over and just waiting, just begging, pleading, to be pinched.

Well, we couldn't let you down, now could we?

We sailed out in hot pursuit of the Saucy Squausage on our piece of driftwood, which we thought we'd better give a piraty name, just in keeping with my swashbuckling mood.

What better than the Gulleon?

By standing one behind the other, and fanning out our wings like sails, the breeze puffed out our feathers and blew the Gulleon fast towards the Saucy Squausage and Lionel's yummy, scrummy treasure.

All aboard
the Gulleon!

16

With the harbour now far behind us, the Gulleon was coming alongside the Saucy Squausage. With pride, I reached down into a box and with my beak pulled out a flag. As we came broadside to broadside, I raised that most feared pirate symbol of all above the Gulleon.

I raised the Gull and Crossbones!

From here, we needed very careful planning. For the attack to be a sure success, we had to show restraint and discipline. We had to weigh up our options so that we could seize as much treasure (all right, as much picnic!) as we could and take it back on board the Gulleon before Lionel woke up.

It would be no use at all for the five of us just to dive on board the Saucy Squausage, making a huge hullabaloo and grabbing and swallowing as much grub as our beaks would allow!

So we stood in a line on board the Gulleon, and planned our attack, slowly and sensibly. Then we…..

Well, what do you think?

Well, then we dived aboard the Saucy Squausage, making a massive hullabaloo, grabbing and stealing whatever grub we could lay our beaks on, and swallowing as much as we could gobble and gollop down our gullets in one go.

It was wild!

It was bedlam!

It was terrific!

It was a squawking, squealing, screaming, swashbuckling feathery Gully pirate picnic fest!

It was piracy on the high seas!

We're gulls, right? It's what we do best.

It was piracy on the high seas!

Lionel's dream was slowly turning into a nightmare.

Still asleep, he dreamt that the Saucy Squausage was being attacked by other pirates, and that his pieces of cake and other foody treasures were falling overboard and the ship was taking on water, and that he was sinking into the sea.

This was probably because he actually *was*.

He began to thrash about, smacking and slapping the water and blathering and burbling in his sleep.

'Get off my food, Blackbeard! Avast behind, Honeysuckle! Splice the mainbrace and shiver me timbers and pass me another piece of cake!' he shouted.

Slowly, but surely, he began to wake up. He looked from side to side, and sat up startled, legs astride the lilo, and he began to realise where he was.

'Oh my, I'm adrift on the ocean waves! What's happened? Help! Honeysuckle love! Where's all the sandwiches and drinks and picnic and stuff? I'll starve! I'll get scurvy without me pies!' he screamed.

Then, he saw us.

'Oh, right. Now I get it. I might have known that you flying rats had something to do with this. It's you what grabbed me picnic. Well Captain Lionel of the Saucy Squausage'll teach you lot a lesson!'

Lionel reached into the sea and pulled out a floating squasage (one that he had sat on earlier!), and brandished it around wildly.

'Come on then, you thieving pirate gulls!' he shouted. 'Come and get what's coming to you!!'

Well, blow me down if the princess didn't swoop right down and snatch Lionel's swishing squasage. Now that was *really* swashbuckling!

Lionel, now furious, grabbed a beach spade with a metal blade and wielded it like a cutlass over his head.

The princess proudly flew over to me with the squasage.

'Avast there, you scurvy flying rats! I'll send you all to Davy Jones' larder!' he cursed, and brought it crashing down towards the princess.

I grabbed the squasage which was still in her beak, knowing that she would never let it go, and flew upwards, dragging her behind me, away from the slashing blade of the beach spade.

The princess was very cross, and thought that I had tried to pinch her squasage (now would I do such a thing?), so she swallowed it whole and then gave me a sharp peck on the neck. Nasty, spiteful, vicious creature. After I'd saved her life too!

Lionel hit the lilo with the metal spade, and it split, and the air began to squeal noisily out, and it began to deflate and slowly sink into the sea.

She thought i'd tried to pinch her squasage!

Oh dear!

All the remains of the picnic were pitched into the water.

He splashed and thrashed around, shouting and screaming, as we flew overhead.

'Help! Help! Me pies! Me Cola Coka! Me sandwiches and crisps! Me picnic! Help, save me!'

Lionel reached out and grabbed a large sealed plastic container, still full of sandwiches. He held on to it, and used it as a float, and began to gather all the rest of the bits and pieces together.

Lionel got hold of a kite string, and by jerking it across the surface of the sea, he managed to get enough breeze to send the kite flying high into the air.

It was a nice kite. We flew around and around it, admiring the bright colours and streamers and taking care not to get tangled up in the line.

I must admit that at first I thought that it was rather a strange moment to choose to fly a kite, but then I realised that Lionel was trying to attract attention and get help. He was showing signs of intelligence that I never imagined he possessed!

It was a nice kite...

21

Ashore in the village, Tyrone was munching a nasty pasty, and looking out to sea. He could see a splashing in the water, and the kite and all of us gulls flying around it, and all the other bits and bods bobbing about on the waves.

'Mum!' he called. 'It's our dad. He's fell in the water!'

'No my love,' said Honeysuckle. 'You means daddy *has fallen* in the water.'

She carried on licking her ice cream.

'All right then. Daddy has fallen in the water! Aren't you going to get him rescued?' he said.

Honeysuckle took another lick.

'Whatever,' she said. 'Where is he anyway?'

'Out there!' shouted the boy frantically, pointing way beyond the harbour walls and headland. 'See! Where those gulls are!'

'Oh yeah. Here, has he got his trunks on, or is he in his flabby old pants like when he sunbathes in the garden? Disgusting….'

'Mum!'

'Well, what's he doing out there? What's the matter with him? Just because he didn't want to share his picnic; how greedy!' said Honeysuckle.

'Mum, he's in trouble!' said Tyrone.

'What, you mean he's finished all his pies? He'll have to eat the sandwiches instead!' she said.

'No! I mean that he could drown. He's drifting off!' said Tyrone.

'Well, why didn't you say so? I'll call for the lifeboat!'

Honeysuckle ran, teetering on her high heels, to the lifeboat house, and within a minute a maroon (which is like a small rocket) was fired. It was used to alert all the lifeboat men that someone needed rescuing.

There was, as usual, a huge bang as the maroon exploded in the sky high over the village, and all the gulls of the village flew up screaming and screeching and wheeling into the air.

Hearing the bang, the lifeboat crew came running into the lifeboat house and pulled on their waterproofs and lifejackets, and in no time at all the lifeboat was speeding out to sea to rescue Lionel.

Now all this is very well, and no matter how nasty and greedy Lionel was he of course had to be rescued, but I have to say that I found the big bang a bit of a nuisance.

You see, all those inquisitive and downright nosey gulls that were now flying high up over the village watched the lifeboat as it sped out towards Lionel and more to the point, *our* floating picnic!

Well, you know how greedy *some* gulls are!

The lifeboat sped out towards us!

I knew that they wouldn't be able to resist flying out to where we were and pinching the picnic that we had just pinched from Lionel, and as I watched, a huge swarm of hungry seagulls flew out after the lifeboat and towards us.

So, as Lionel splashed and floundered around amidst the floating buckets and spades and flasks and sandwiches, we left the safety of the Gulleon and paddled over and began to eat as much of the leftovers of the floating pirate picnic as quickly as we possibly could.

There was no time to loose. No time to be choosy. Everything, but everything, had to go.

No problem.

We're gulls, right?

It's what we do!

We were so concentrating on stuffing and gorging ourselves that we hardly noticed as the lifeboat arrived, and the crew hauled Lionel out of the sea and into the safety of the boat.

They handed Lionel a lifejacket and told him to put it on. He couldn't get it over his head. The three crewmen held him down and together prodded and pulled and pushed with the straps and buckles of the lifejacket.

'Here mate,' pleaded Lionel from the bottom of the boat, red faced and half strangled by a strap. 'Hang on a minute. There's a pie floating over there, and a bag of cheese and onion crisps, and a barbeque chicken wing and a couple of boiled eggs, in mayonnaise I think. It'll all sink! It'll be a tragedy, especially the pie. It's a steak and kidney. Hadn't you better rescue them as well?'

There was no need for Lionel to have worried. Black Annie and Snitch and Snatch and the princess and I 'rescued' all the food.

Oh yes, we rescued it in our stomachs, and soon it was all safe and sound! Kindly, we left just a few crumbs and crisps and bits and pieces for all the other gulls to scrap over, just to show them what they had missed.

We watched them from the Gulleon.

How they squabbled and fought and scrapped! I had never, ever before seen so many gulls fight over such a tiny amount of food. It was so undignified.

In a short while they had got rid of every single little morsel and then, as one, they rose and flew up from the sea and flocked back towards the village.

It was time for us to do the same.

I stretched my wings and flapped.

And flapped.

And flapped.

So did the princess and the others.

We didn't move at all. We just couldn't take off!

Slowly it dawned on me that after eating all that floating picnic, even if my wings were as wide as those of an albatross, I could never have got off the ground.

It was impossible.

And so it was for the princess and Black Annie and Snitch and Snatch.

We looked at one another. We couldn't fly and we were adrift on the Gulleon on the high seas!

The lifeboat crew had at last finished pulling the lifejacket on Lionel. One of the crew spotted us adrift on the Gulleon.

'Here,' he said. 'Isn't that those gulls from Mrs Baker's roof on that piece of driftwood, next to those two young ones? That one with the ring on his leg and his mate. And the big one-eyed, one-legged Black Annie from the beach? They look like they're having trouble flying.'

'Yeah, good!' said Lionel. 'Blooming stinking gulls pinched me picnic, they did. Go on, let 'em float off out to sea. That'll teach 'em!'

I saw the piece of string that earlier we'd thought was a strand of spaghetti. It was floating next to the Gulleon. I leaned over the side and plucked it from the sea, and held it in my beak.

'Look at that,' said the crewman to his mate. 'He's holding that piece of string in his beak. Grab the other end!'

His mate grabbed the string.

'Hooray!' cheered Lionel. 'What are you going to do? Strangle them with it? That's the way! Horrible thieving flying rats!'

'Oh no,' said the crewman. 'We lifeboatmen save lives, and if it hadn't been for these gulls flying up above you, we'd never have spotted you in the first place! You'd be drifting halfway across the sea to America. You should thank those gulls for saving your life.'

Lionel sneered at us. Well…how ungrateful can you get?

The crewman held onto one end of the string in his hand, and I held the other in my beak, and they towed us and the Gulleon all the way back, safely into the harbour.

Phew!

That was the luckiest escape I've had for years.

The lifeboat brought us in, and the Gulleon washed up on the beach and we all

That was the luckiest escape I've had for years

hopped off. Still stuffed full of picnic, the princess and I waddled across the sand and pebbles back towards the gullery.

The princess looked at me.

'Gully' she said. 'I'm sorry I pecked you earlier on. You saved me from getting chopped in half by the spade, didn't you?'

'Well, yes,' I said.

'And you were clever enough to get us a tow back with the lifeboat.'

'Yes'

She smiled.

'My pirate king, my Gully,' she said, and looked down.

In front of her on the roof lay a lovely, juicy squasage. But this was more than an ordinary squasage; this was a squasage of undying true love and respect and affection, this was a seafaring, swashbuckling squausage, this was….

This was very similar to the squasage that I thought she had swallowed so greedily earlier on. Very, very similar indeed….

Almost identical in fact…..

Virtually impossible to tell them apart…

'My hero!' she said.

'And I thought that you'd swallowed it…' I said.

'Of course not, my sweet,' she said. 'I could never be so greedy. I hid it under my wing for you.'

Isn't she clever? I'd never have guessed….well, I'm only a gull, right?

"And I thought you'd swallowed it!" I said.

The other misadventures
of the wicked seagull

Also available three mischievous adventures
of the wicked seagull on CD

Other books Celebrity Chef and Gully Goes Green

Visit the website to see the full range of Gully books and merchandise

www.thegullery.co.uk

Or phone The Gullery on 01208 880937

The Author

The creator, author and illustrator
of Gully, Jon Cleave, lives in the
heart of the lovely old Cornish
fishing village of Port Isaac with
his wife Caroline and boys Jakes,
George and Theo.... oh yes, and
hundreds and hundreds
of squealing, squawking,
screaming seagulls!